11/99

Disco

Joseph Brodsky

pictures by Vladimir Radunsky

Farrar Straus Giroux   New York

In the beginning there were just waves
hammering at the obstacles.
The stars were starring to constant raves
but had no Oscars.

The clouds would go a bit further and
frequently act impertinent,
which was self-destructive, and downpours meant
obscurity to the continent.

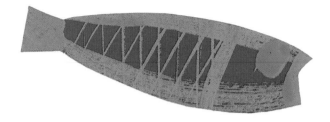

America first was discovered by fish.
But, far from being eternal
and often making a tasty dish,
fish normally keep no journal.

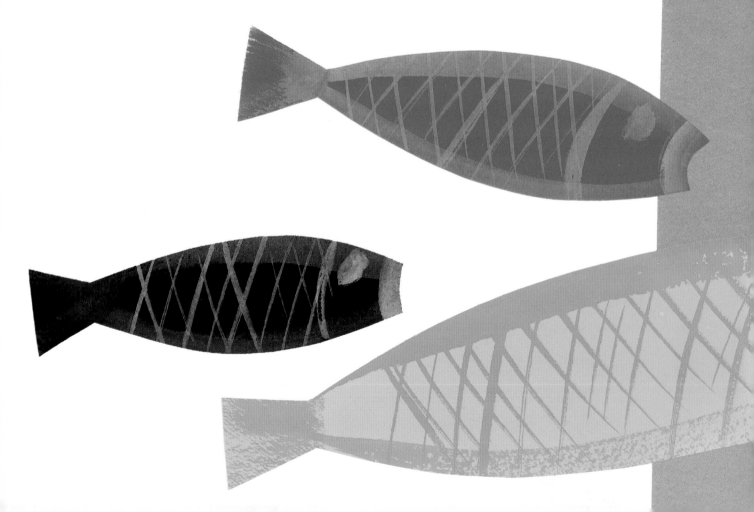

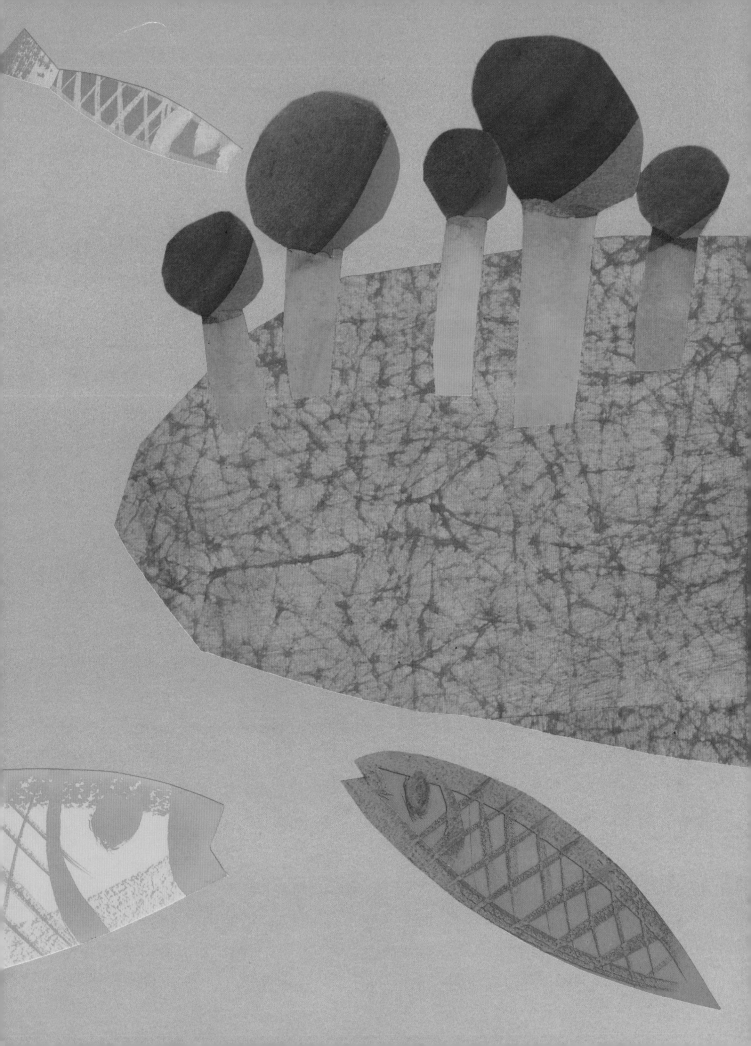

Then birds discovered America, too—
the screeching seagulls and petrels.
Yet they were just pilgrims, and very few
of them evolved into settlers.

So for millions of years or—as some insist—
longer, Nature played prudent:
on one hand, America would exist;
on the other, it wouldn't.

Still, this bothered America little, since
it knew no public mention.
When you are a continent, you don't mince
words and don't crave attention.

So then Nature sat down and picked up her pen
to make what fish and seagull
saw a reality: off sailed men
and made America legal.

They stepped ashore and they rode across
this land of milk and honey,
and they settled it with their many laws,
their cities, their farms, their money.

BANK

MONEY

Now America has all its maps and charts:
they would fill up your barn and cupboard.
But do you believe in your heart of hearts
that America was discovered?

Don't you think that this land still has a few
secrets? That, huge and silent,
it waits for their being discovered by you,
since Nature is out on assignment?

Distributed in Canada by Douglas & McIntyre Ltd.

Color separations by Hong Kong Scanner Arts. Printed and bound in the United States of America by Berryville Graphics. First edition, 1999